Chuck's Dinosaur Tinglers
Volume 1

CHUCK TINGLE

Copyright © 2015 Chuck Tingle

All rights reserved.

ISBN: 1507794185
ISBN-13: 978-1507794180

You are the soul of books.

- Chuck Tingle

CONTENTS

Acknowledgments i

1 My Billionaire Triceratops Craves Gay Ass 1

2 Gay T-Rex Law Firm: Executive Boner 12

3 Space Raptor Butt Invasion 22

ACKNOWLEDGMENTS

Thank you to my son, Jon Tingle, for editing all my books. You get all the ladies and I look up to you a lot.

No thanks to Ted Cobbler from down the street. He drives too fast like he owns the whole block.

MY BILLIONAIRE TRICERATOPS CRAVES GAY ASS

I hadn't seen Oliver, my pet triceratops, in years, but what I remember about him wasn't great. While my other pets were easy going and free spirited, he was the voice of discipline and reason. A large creature with broad shoulders and a deep, bellowing voice, I eventually become more than a little scared of him, and eventually thankful when he finally moved to the deep south to become a dancer at an all male cabaret. I couldn't discipline him either, as he had become a billion due to string of impeccably well-placed Super Bowl bets.

All the while, though, I kept a secret regarding Oliver bottled up deep inside, pushed deep into the darkest corners of my brain and only brought out sparingly in my weakest, lustful gay moments. It was dark, forbidden fantasy I wouldn't dare tell a soul and had trouble even admitting to myself.

For as much of an overbearing pain in the ass that my gay billionaire triceratops was, I always thought he was kind of hot. Incredibly hot, actually, if we're going to be honest.

Of course, those days I was still buried deep within the closet, anyway, and as far as I knew triceratops and human relationship rarely ever worked. He hasn't been a part of my life for a long time, showing up on my doorstep without a penny to his name just four years back, so it's nothing I have to worry about.

These day's I'm living on the East Coast, after falling in love with New York during my college years away from home. My family is still in Los Angeles but I see them frequently, sometimes making the flight back for the holidays and other times hosting them on trips to the big apple. I love my family, but enjoy living far away and having the space to grow and make my own choices, my own mistakes, without the ever-present eye of my mother, siblings, or gay triceratops.

I'm sitting up on the roof of my apartment building, watching the sunset through the towering skyscrapers that consume the purple and orange skyline. It's one of those gorgeous New York evenings that has to be experienced first hand to completely understand; the way the cool air tickles your skin from over the ocean, the electric hum of the people below and the lives intersecting in any number of ways. It's as if anything could happen at any moment, the calm before the storm. I've been drinking and feel sufficiently relaxed after a long day at work, but my mellow silence is broken unexpectedly by the phone vibrating in my pocket.

I pull it out and immediately notice that it's an unknown number, which is almost as weird as someone calling instead of texting. I'd usually just ignore the call, but I'm feeling particularly adventurous today and decide to pick up.

"Hello?" I ask, putting the phone up to my ear and leaning back into my chair.

"Jeremy?"

I recognize the voice immediate and sit straight up. It's been years, but it'd know that deep dinosaur tone anywhere.

"Holy shit." I laugh, still in shock. "Is this Oliver?"

"I've missed you a lot, Jeremy." Oliver says, a deep pain in his voice.

"I know." I tell him as a single tear wells up and rolls down my cheek. I wasn't prepared for this just of conversation tonight. "I've missed you too."

The conversation almost immediately goes silent, neither of us knowing exactly what to say next. Suddenly, the ever-present sound of traffic and car horns from the streets below seems lonely and homesick. I used to hate this dinosaur nuisance, breathing a sight of relief when he first left, but for some reason I'm incredibly glad that he called.

"Everything okay?" Oliver's voice asks from the other end of the line, knocking me back into reality. "Sorry, it's kinda hard to hold the phone up with my claws."

"Oh, yeah." I stammer, "Everything's great."

"Good, good." He says, awkwardly. "So anyway, I know it's been a while but I'm in town dancing and your mom said that you were in the city now."

I laugh. "You talked to my mom?"

"Well, you know." Oliver admits. "It was probably right when you moved here but I figured I'd look you up on the off chance you were still around."

"Yep." I say, "I'm still here trying to make it work."

"Yeah, I hear you." Oliver says. "Its hard right now, the cabaret isn't looking good at all but luckily I still have all my Super Bowl winnings."

I scoff. "I figured as much. You've got no room to complain, rich ass dinosaur."

As I take another long swig of beer I feel something strange and dangerous brewing within me, an anxious ache that I can't quite put my finger on but is certainly there, and more than a little terrifying. I immediately push it away and pretend that the feeling never occurred, but I can't deny that for a brief moment it was there in the pit of my stomach.

"I've got tomorrow night off." Oliver says. "I was thinking maybe I could take you out to dinner and we could catch up."

I sigh. "I don't know, I'm pretty busy these days."

Oliver has been around long enough not to growl or roar when someone turns him down, even his former owner. He's a triceratops who's aged to perfection and has all of the confidence and charm that comes with it. He doesn't need me. "Alright," Oliver says without a second thought. "No worries."

Almost immediately I regret my reaction. "Wait."

"Yes?"

"I think I can make something work," I tell him. "There's a nice restaurant a few blocks from my place that I've been hoping to try. It's called The Chow Lounge. Want to meet me there?"

"How's eight?" Oliver asks.

"I can do that." I tell him. "I'll see you then."

"See you then, buddy." Oliver says before hanging up, leaving me alone once again on the rooftop. A strange current runs through my blood, an excitement that I don't want to admit to myself.

I close my eyes as the sun finally dips completely behind the edge of the earth.

I show up at the restaurant a little bit late but immediately spot Oliver, who's sitting quietly at a table in a dark corner of the room. The place is beautiful and much more expensive than anywhere I'd go on my own, but I'm more than certain Oliver is paying so why not spring on something nice. He stands up to greet me as I walk over to him, giving me a big hug with his tiny triceratops arm and then pulling out my chair as I sit down in the across from him; Old school Jurassic chivalry.

The dim, romantic lighting is enough to make anyone look sexy, but Oliver has clearly aged beautifully. He was always a good-looking dinosaur, but the specks of grey that now dot his scales have added an air of self-assured beastliness. Oliver's also dressed way been then he ever did when he was my pet, the cutthroat world of male burlesque doing a complete one-eighty on his previously tired fashion sense.

He sits down and smiles wide with a mouthful of sharp teeth. "Whoa. Look at you, Jeremy."

"Here I am." I laugh with an uncomfortable shrug.

"You look handsome." Oliver offers. "I can't believe this. When's the last time I saw you?"

I think for a moment, trying to count the years. "four years, maybe?"

Oliver nods. "That sounds about right."

We sit in silence for a moment as my mind races. Oliver doesn't seem uncomfortable at all, however, completely in control of the situation, which unfortunately makes him seem even sexier. I know I'm not supposed to think these taboo gay thoughts about my own dinosaur pet, but I can't deny the attraction that so blatantly bubbles right below the surface. It's so wrong, and I'd never act on it, but I know that it's there.

"Where are you working?" Oliver asks.

"I'm at a production house." I tell him. "Editing commercials."

A huge smile crosses his triceratops face. "Really? Oh that's great. Remember those movies you used to make and show everybody?"

I laugh at this reminder of my former hobby. "How could I forget?"

"Those were great." Oliver tells me. "You were a natural, I guess it makes a lot of sense for you to be doing that stuff now."

I nod. A waiter comes by to ask us if we'd like anything to drink, and I start to decline but Oliver immediately swings into action, ordering us a remarkably nice bottle of wine. The waiter nods at me and the dinosaur and leaves.

"Whoa! What are we celebrating?" I ask, jokingly.

"This! I haven't seen my owner in seven years!" Oliver exclaims. "Bring on the wine! This is a big night for a former pet!"

I laugh and shake my head in amusement. It's weird to be here as a peer with someone who had always been just a dinosaur companion to me. I would have never dreamed that one day we would be sharing a glass of wine at a fancy restaurant like two grown adults.

"You didn't tell your mom you were meeting up with me, did you?" He asks, a hint of something pensive and weird in his voice.

"Ha! No." I tell him. "Are you kidding me? She was never happy about taking you in when we were back home. I don't think she'd be happy with me still talking to a dinosaur... no offence."

Oliver shakes his head. "None taken, I understand. It's hard to get people to see past the scales, especially when raptors and t-rexes are out there messing it up for the rest of us."

The wine comes and Oliver tries a sip with his large mouth, then approves. The waiter pours us each a glass and takes our order, which amounts to a salad for me and a steak for Oliver.

"You have a girlfriend?" Oliver asks as the waiter leaves.

"No." I tell him.

He eyes me for a moment. "Boyfriend?"

I laugh. "No, but you're getting warmer now."

Oliver shakes his head and smiles. "That's hard to believe." He confesses. "Look at you! My god, you're a good looking guy. Fucking sexy and finally out of the closet."

"Oliver!" I shout. "You can't say that!"

He bursts out laughing. "What? I'm not your pet anymore! I can say these things if I want to, and besides it's the truth." He leans in closer. "You know, half the people in here probably think we're on a date, anyway. Some rich old triceratops with a hot piece of human arm candy."

I glance around the restaurant and suddenly realize that he's probably right. As taboo as dinosaur human relationships are, they're still not entirely unheard of, especially here in the big city.

I take a deep breath. "Do you want me to be your arm candy?" I ask him.

The second that the words leave my lips I can't believe I actually asked them. My face immediately flushes as I wait for his response, and I can't help but glance down at my half finished glass of wine.

Suddenly, his claw crosses the table and covers my own. A sensual chill immediately runs down my spine as my eyes look back up to meet his.

"I'd like that." Oliver says.

I wait before speaking again, my heart racing in my chest.

"This is trouble." I tell him.

"Is it?" Oliver says. "Sometimes trouble can be a lot of fun."

I hesitate for a moment, my eyes lingering on the shape of his large manly horns. "Would you like to see my place after dinner?" I ask.

He smiles. "How about right now? Suddenly, I'm not so hungry."

"We just ordered." I protest.

Oliver stands up and heads over to the hostess. They chat for a moment and then he walks back to the table and confidently offers a claw. "It's all taken care of."

The next thing I know, the triceratops and I are briskly strolling the streets of Manhattan back towards my apartment. Neither of us speaks a word, but our own thoughts are more than busy enough to keep us occupied. I know exactly what's going to happen when we get upstairs, and my body is literally trembling with anticipation. Everything about this is so wrong, but it feels so right.

I reach the front door of my building and fumble while punching in the number, my hands literally shaking too much to function properly. I try again and screw up a second time, pressing pound before the code instead of after.

"Everything okay there?" Oliver asks. "This is your place right? You're not just trying to break in?"

I laugh nervously. Luckily, someone exits the building while I'm making my third attempt and we slip inside, then we head straight for the elevator.

"I'm excited to see your place." Oliver tells me coolly as the elevator doors close and it shoots upward, his massive dinosaur body taking up most of the space inside.

I give Oliver a smile, not sure how to respond.

Finally, the lift stops and the doors open. I lead the way down the hall and then stop at my apartment, feeling Oliver's looming presence behind me as I insert my key and push open the door. We step inside and immediately he is upon me, turning me around and pushing me hard up against the wall of the entryway.

His claws roam my body freely as he kisses me hard, smelling a familiar dinosaur scent I haven't thought of in years. Oliver's scales feel rough but pleasant against my face, a reminder of his beastly dominance as he takes my hands and pushes them back above my head. I whimper softly, trying to hold onto a shred of protest but I simply can't do it. This is exactly what I want, exactly what I've always wanted but been to afraid to admit it.

Oliver feverishly starts to unbutton my shirt but it's taking too long so he eventually tears it off in a spray of tiny white buttons, revealing my toned young chest underneath.

My hands have taken on a mind of their own at this point, running up and down his body and pulling his shirt from his large dinosaur pants. I rub my fingers across Oliver's toned abs, even more impressive than the last time I saw them on our family vacation to Greece.

"You've been working out." I manage to say through the flurry of kisses.

"Dancing." He responds. "It's good for a dinosaur's bod."

I immediately start to unbutton his pants and thrust my hand inside, grabbing hold of his rock hard dick. Oliver is fully engorged and his cock is absolutely massive, taunting me as I pull it from its cloth sheath. I grasp his dick firmly and stroke with slow, deliberate movements. He starts to push back against me, finding a rhythm within my fingers.

"You've been a bad boy, haven't you?" Oliver asks me between frantic kisses.

"Yeah." I moan. "I need to be taught a lesson."

The next thing I know, Oliver is pushing me down towards the floor. I drop to my knees and suddenly I'm faced with his enormous cock, which I promptly take into my mouth. He stretches my lips tight with the girth of his giant dino member, pushing me up and down on his length while I struggle to consume him.

Eventually, Oliver drives down hard and forces his dick up against the limits of my gag reflex. I try my best to take him but fumble, retching as the mammoth cock chokes me. I pull him out with a gasp, coughing and sputtering.

"You need to do as I tell you." The billionaire dinosaur demands, standing above me in towering authority. "And I'm telling you to swallow my fucking cock."

"I'm sorry, sir." I say, looking up at him through watery eyes.

I open my mouth wide and try again, relaxing as much as I can as Oliver slides his cock back down into my depths. This time I'm ready for him, and as his dick plunges deeper I somehow manage to accommodate his size, allowing him to plummet well below my gag reflex. Oliver lets out a loud roar of pleasure as he reaches the bottom, his green balls resting tightly against my chin and holding there.

Just as I'm about the run out of air Oliver lets me up again, but only long enough to survive because seconds later he's pushing me back down onto his cock. This time the movements are rapid and powerful, forcing me up and down on his length with brutal strength. He's completely dinohandling me and I love every second of it, the domination filling my body with a strange lustful desire. I'm rock hard, and as he pummels my throat with his massive dick I reach down and slide my hand into my pants. My cock is swollen and sensitive to my own firm touch, aching as I rub it in time with the movements between my lips.

Finally, I'm just too horny to take it any longer. I pull Oliver out of my mouth and the desperately command. "Fuck me right now. I need you in my asshole with that triceratops dick!"

Oliver smiles and lifts me to my feet. "With pleasure."

"Punish me." I beg. "I've been a bad, bad boy."

The next thing I know we are stumbling through my apartment, finally landing on the couch that sits directly in the center of my living room. I climb up onto it on all fours as Oliver tears down my pants and the tight black briefs beneath.

As the cool air hits my skin I shiver with excitement. I had no idea things would ever go this far, and now that they have I feel like I'm on a rollercoaster with no breaks. This moment has been building for years and now that it's finally here I don't know how to react, completely overwhelmed by my homosexual taboo attraction to this ferocious dinosaur.

I look back over my shoulder at Oliver, who has stripped naked and stands confidently behind me, aligning his massive cock with my tightness.

"Tell me I'm a nasty human manslut." I beg.

Oliver shakes his head in mock disappointment. "What are we going to do with you? Such a nasty little human twink, you need a real dinosaur to show you how to fuck."

"I'm sorry." I say, biting my lip coyly.

"Sorry isn't good enough this time you fucking human slutboy." My triceratops roars. "You're going to take this dick until you can't even walk straight."

"I deserve it." I tell him. "I deserve to be punished."

"Yes you do." Oliver agrees.

With that, he thrusts forward into my asshole and stretches me out brutally. I let out a yelp of unexpected pleasure as he filled me up, reeling from the sensation as Oliver starts to push in and out of me.

"Oh fuck." I moan. "You're so fucking big."

Oliver slaps my ass hard. "Say it again."

"Your dinosaur cock is so fucking big!" I scream, gripping the couch tightly in front of me. I'm not lying either. Everything about Oliver is huge, from the size of his dick to the width of he powerful legs as he grabs me by the waist and propels me back and forth on his cock.

Eventually, he starts to pick up the pace, his movements slowly evolving into a rapid-fire slam against my ass. He feels incredible inside of me, now a seasoned gay lover who knows exactly where to thrust within a man. I can feel a prostate orgasm slowly creeping its way across my body, pulsing inside of me with more and more power until finally it explodes across me in a sensual wave. My quiet trembling instantly becomes a violent quake as my muscles contract wildly, jizz ejecting from the head of my cock. I throw my head back and let out a frantic howl of pleasure.

All the while, Oliver doesn't let up for a second, absolutely pummeling me from behind with all of his monsterous strength. When the orgasm finally passes he immediately grabs me and lifts me up, carrying my small body across the apartment and kicking open the door to my bedroom. There, he throws me onto the bed, where I lay on my back and lift my legs up into the air.

Oliver climbs into position and then pushes his swollen dino dick back inside of me with a low groan, immediate getting back to work. From this angle I can see his incredible body, toned and muscular due to a rigid dance routine that could only be accomplished by the most disciplined of prehistoric creatures. I reach down and run my hands across his impeccable abs, my cock already starting to stiffen again.

"You're not used to getting fucked by a real dinosaur are you?" Oliver asks. "The human guys just can't keep up with this."

I shake my head in agreement. "They don't ever fuck me like this." I tell him. "They don't have your massive triceracock!"

Oliver takes one of my muscular legs in each hand and spreads them wide, testing the limits of my flexibility. My twice-weekly yoga classes have clearly been paying off and I handle it with no problem, giving him a little wink as he pummels my asshole without mercy.

Eventually, Oliver pulls out of me and pauses for a moment, catching his breath.

"What is it?" I ask.

"It's time for your real punishment." Oliver says.

"Oh no." I say with a smile. "What are you going to do with me?"

I can see Oliver reach over and grab something off of my dresser, I large black dildo that I like to keep handy for those lonely nights in. Oliver slips the dildo casually into my ass, but suddenly I feel the head of his cock pressed firmly against the door of my asshole as well. I gasp.

"Double penetration? I've never done that before." I admit.

"Well then who better to teach you then your favorite billionaire pet?" Oliver offers.

The words sizzle against my skin, so hot and so wrong. I can't believe how depraved I've become as the night continues on, because at this point I'll do anything that he wants me to.

"Double fuck my ass with your cock and that dildo." I beg. "Teach me how it's done."

"Well, first you relax." Oliver tells me. He pushes forward even more, the pressure building but the tight rim of my hole still maintaining its integrity. "Relax, Jeremy."

I close my eyes and reach down with one hand to play with my cock, focusing on the deep, primal sound of Oliver's voice.

Suddenly, I feel the limits of my asshole give way as the enormous dildo slides in next to Oliver's member, stretching me out with its incredible thickness.

"Fuck!" I shout in a mixture of pleasure and pain. I quickly gain speed with the rapid strokes across my dick, trying to somehow balance out all of the peculiar sensations at work within my body. Oliver pumps slowly at first, driving his cock up into me with a deliberate, sensual movement, but as we continue he grows faster and faster until eventually he's pounding me up the ass with all of his force.

I can feel myself edging towards a second orgasm now as a familiar warmth begins to grow inside of me. I clench my teeth tight and brace for the powerful surge that I know is coming right around the corner, but no amount of anticipation can prepare me for the explosion of pleasure when it hits. My eyes roll back into my head and I scream a blood-curling scream, my back arching like a demon mid-exorcism. I immediately lose grasp on where I am and what I'm doing, becoming nothing more than a ball of hot white bliss. Cum shoots out of my cock in a series of thick milky ropes.

Oliver is still pounding away ruthlessly, but my shrieking troughs of passion must have sent him over the edge because suddenly he is lifting me up in the air once again. The dildo pops out. My legs spread wide, the triceratops impales my tiny frame onto his towering rod of a cock, using gravity to force me down even harder than before over his dino dick.

I'm completely maxed out and blathering like a mindless gay sex friend when Oliver starts to cum as well. I can feel the muscles in his arms contract as he pushes and holds deep within my asshole, ejecting a series of hot white payloads up my butt.

"Oh my fucking god!" Oliver yells. I can feel every pulse of his cock as his jizz shoots up inside of me, filling me to the brim and then squirting out from the corners of my plugged asshole. It drips onto the floor below in warm, pearly splatters as I hang there in his arms.

When all of the semen has finally been drained from Oliver's giant cock, he carefully removes himself from me and places me back on the bed, where the two of us stare blankly at each other's nude and fucked senseless bodies. A few seconds pass in silence until a smile slow creeps across my face and I burst out laughing.

"What's so funny?" Oliver asks.

"Nothing." I say. "How did we end up here?"

Oliver leans back against my dresser and rests, his chest still heaving from the ferocious sexual workout.

"Chemistry is chemistry." He tells me. "Dinosaur, human, whatever."

I laugh. "You're right about that."

GAY T-REX LAW FIRM: EXECUTIVE BONER

"I see that you've done secretarial work before. It was at another law firm?" The T-rex across the desk from me asks. "Two years of experience there?"

"Yes" I tell him, trying to hide the nervous waver in my voice. "A small one."

"And why did you leave?"

"Well, I just didn't see my work leading anywhere. I'm from a small town, and the firm wasn't quite as fulfilling as a firm like this one is." I tell him, glancing around the massive office that I sit in, the New York skyline stretching out forever in the windows behind me. "I wanted to do more with myself."

"You have a law degree, though." The T-rex says, as if I didn't already know this.

"Yes." I nod.

"So why are you applying for the secretary position?" He questions.

"Jobs are hard to find these days, even with my qualifications. I'm just happy to be applying for a job with one of the leading law offices in all of New York City. It's an honor to be inside this building."

The T-rex nods slightly, his eyes still scanning over my resume. He's incredibly hard to read, sharp and focused. His lips form a tight line across his expressionless dinosaur face.

My heart is pounding out of my chest.

"Okay, just a few more questions." He finally says. "Have you ever worked for a dinosaur before?"

I shake my head. "No sir, but I'm excited about the prospect."

With this, the T-rex raps on the table with his tiny little hand and stands up quickly. "Please excuse me," He says. "I'll be right back." Seconds later, he's gone, leaving me to sit alone in his bright luxurious office.

The room is beautifully furnished with a modern flair, a minimalist workspace that would look perfectly at home in an architecture or contemporary design magazine.

Moments later the T-rex reenters, not wasting any time. "Alright Donny, you're the man we've been looking for. Welcome to Jurassic Law."

I stand up in complete shock, having thoroughly convinced myself that this interview was going terribly. I shake the T-rex's hand, briefly taking note of how cold his scaled skin is. "Thank you very much, sir."

"You'll start tomorrow morning." He tells me.

As if my interview wasn't nerve wrecking enough, the first day of work I'm a living, breathing ball of stress. I'm dressed as professional as I can muster without looking twenty years older than I actually am, a sleek black suit and my dark hair parted neatly to the side.

I look good and I know it, a young, fresh-faced guy in the big city. But today I'll need a little more help than that, Jurassic Law is notoriously hard for humans to gain any respect around the office.

I scan my keycard in the building lobby then hop inside an elevator and quickly punch the button for floor ten. As the door begins to close a T-rex in a grey suit picks up his pace and slips inside.

"You must be Donny." He says, extending his clawed dino-hand. "I'm Tyson, Tyson Rex. Very nice too meet you."

I shake his hand. "Nice to meet you too, Tyson." I tell him.

"I guess I'm your new boss." He says with a laugh as the elevator shoots upwards. "I'll show you to your desk."

We reach our floor and step out into a bustling office. Tyson leads me past the front check-in and down through a large series of corridors until we reach the main room, which is mostly a long series of desks and doors leading to the various partners at the firm. Each desk has a T-rex answering phones and taking messages, all of them apparently very busy this morning. As we walk past them I receive a series of looks that could only be described as awkward, me being the new human and all, but I don't have enough time to really consider them because moments later we are at the end of the room in front of an empty chair. Two large double doors stand menacingly nearby.

"This is your office?" I ask, nodding at the doors.

Tyson nods. "Yes."

"How'd you get such a nice one?" I joke.

"I'm senior partner." He tells me in complete deadpan.

My face turns bright red. "Sorry, sir." I sit down in the empty chair and start straightening things out as Tyson bursts out laughing.

"It's okay!" He says. "Don't worry about it, I know it's going to take you a few days to get the hang of things around here but it's all pretty simple."

After giving me a brief rundown Tyson retreats back into his office though the large double doors, leaving me to sit in front of a whole pile of unorganized papers that wait to be filed. I take a deep breath and then clear my thoughts, time to get to work.

The minutes slowly turn into hours and somehow the stack of things that I need to organize seems to grow larger and larger as I go, thanks mostly to the continuous delivery of more and more paperwork from office curriers throughout the day. I feel like I am drowning in paper, trying and failing to stay above the constant stream of white rectangles.

What's even more frustrating though, is that it seems like all of the other secretaries are doing just fine. As the evening grows later I glance down the row of desks and realize that several of the other workers, both human and Tyrannosaur alike, have already left and gone home, finished with the day's organizational duties.

"Sorry." A mail boy interrupts my train of thought as he drops off yet another stack of papers on the desk.

"Are you fucking kidding me?" I snap at him.

The guy says nothing, just turns around and hurries away. Behind him I can see the sun disappearing slowly over the horizon line, a beautifully frustrating scene.

"Fuck." I say to myself, lowering my head onto the stack of papers in exhaustion. I lay there for a moment and let my eyelids slip closed and my breathing slow. Just a few moments of rest, I think. The bustling sounds of the office slip farther and farther away as I relax and let my worries drift. I'm sinking into the darkness, letting it envelope me in it's warm, peaceful embrace.

"Donny?" A deep voice says from behind me, a cool claw on my shoulder.

My eyes shoot open. The office is completely dark and empty, the only dim lighting to been seen is courtesy of the long row of screen savers on the computers to my right. I quickly sit up, realizing that I'd fallen asleep. Tyson stands behind me.

"I'm so sorry, sir." I say in a panic. "I didn't mean to fall asleep, I just..." The words trail off.

"That's okay." Tyson tells me calmly, "I was planning to keep you late, anyway."

"What?" I ask, confused.

"Procedure." Tyson explains. "It's what we do on the first day for your position."

"But why?" I stammer.

"Well, to test your commitment." Tyson laughs a deep dinosaur laugh as he says this. "You think you're going to have this much paperwork to file every day? No."

"That's a little sadistic, isn't it?" I venture, slightly pissed off now.

"Well, we are carnivores." Tyson smiles, showing two glinting rows of dagger like teeth. He pulls out a chair across from me and sits down, face to face. "What do you want?" He asks.

"Right now?"

"From this job."

I think about his question for a moment and then finally answer. "Stability. A steady paycheck."

Tyson nods. "It's always greed with you humans isn't it?"

"Well, no."

"That's okay." Tyson nods in assurance. "That's probably the most common one. Now how much money are we talking here?"

"How much money?"

"A million dollars? Two million dollars? What would be enough for you?"

I laugh. "That's my salary?"

"No," Tyson tells me, putting a claw over my hand. "It's a one time payment, it needs to last."

I shrug. "Okay, ten million dollars then." I throw out the first number that comes to mind.

Tyson smiles. "Great." The next thing I know, Tyson is opening a briefcase and pulling out what appears to be some sort of legal document. He hands it to me and I read aloud.

"Contract to run a T-rex gangbang train on Donny Sullivan's gay human ass for the sum of ten million dollars even." I can hardly say it with a straight face. "Is this a joke? What is this?"

"Exactly what it looks like."

"But I'm not gay!" I protest, shaking my head. "You want me to sign this?"

"That's up to you." Tyson says. "You're providing a service to us, and in return we will provide a service to you, in the form of ten million dollars."

Finally, I've had enough. I'm exhausted after such a long evening and as much as I appreciate a good practical joke on the first day, this whole game is wearing thin. I'm not going to lose it on Tyson because, after all, he's my boss, but that doesn't mean I'm not over it and ready to head home.

"Whatever." I tell him, grabbing a pen and scribbling my name across the bottom line. "I need to get back to my apartment."

The second that my pen leaves the page my T-rex boss stands up from his chair. "Follow me." Tyson instructs.

I want to tell him that I need to get home, that I'm tired and sore and overworked, but it's the first day of work and I'm not about to disobey my superior. He was joking with that contract, right? A little bit of dinosaur on human humor?

I stand up and walk slowly towards the double doors as Tyson follows behind. Terror fills my brain, an instinctual realization that something is terribly wrong. I've gotten in way over my head with these tyrannosaurs rex lawyers.

As I move closer and closer the door slowly creeks open on it's own, revealing a large boardroom with an enormous oak table positioned in the center off it. Surrounding the table are several dinosaurs, dressed to the nines in suit and ties, watching hungrily as I approach while in the back of the room a fireplace roars. It's terrifyingly full of rippling red flames. Tyson follows closely as the doors close behind me.

"This is Donny!" Tyson announces to the ground. "He's the new human in the office and he's agreed to let is show him how us T-rexes treat greedy little humans on the first day at work."

The group applauds in approval.

When I realize that the contract was not a joke I go into a complete panic. "Wait a minute, you were being serious?" I stammer.

Tyson laughs. "Should have read the fine print, huh? Don't worry, were not going to eat you. It's a sexual transaction, nothing more, nothing less."

I let out a sigh. Guess I'm fucking these dinosaurs tonight.

I begin stripping off my button up shirt and pulling down my slacks. I move slowly and deliberately, revealing the black boxer briefs that were hidden underneath. As my skin hits the warm air I shudder, a chill of arousal running down my spine. On the one hand, being out of my own control is horrifying, yet somehow this situation is also making me incredibly horny. I'd never had a gay experience before, nor did I particularly want to but, now that I couldn't help it, I felt a small spark lighting somewhere deep inside of me.

Once down to my bare essentials, I step forward and climb onto the long, narrow table, making my way across it on hands and knees. The dinosaurs seem to enjoy this, and they begin to stand up from their chairs and gather around me, Tyson included. They gather at the edges of the table, large enough that they tower above me while I crawl, with their green, throbbing T-rex dicks pointing out at me from every direction.

I sit back on my knees and reach out with each hand to grab two of the monstrous shafts. The beasts rear back and moan deeply while I stroke them, reeling from the sensation of my tight grip. Terror fills my entire body, yet I smile up at them and, while screaming on the inside, ask, "You like what a nasty gay boy I am?"

The dinosaurs huff and puff in approval. Eventually, they begin to switch places, taking turns between my fingers until finally one of them has had enough and grabs my head, then forces my mouth down around his gigantic rod. The penetration is unexpected, and I quickly find myself gagging as his thickness presses up against the edge of my gag reflex. Tears well up in my eyes while the T-rex pumps in and out of me until finally he lets me up and I gasp for air, frantically trying to ready myself for the next violation. It comes fast, but this time I'm ready, relaxing my throat and letting his entire length slip down into me, taking him deeper than even I expected I was capable. Eventually, I find my face pressed against his green, toned abs, lapping at his balls with my tongue like a puppy while I deep throat his cock. The beast pumps up and down, fucking my face until finally passing me onto the next one in line, who quickly picks up where the last left off.

The prehistoric monsters continue like this for quite a while, treating me like a gay human sex toy, then finally one of them grabs me by the ass and spins me around on the table. He takes my boxer briefs and tears them off in one firm rip, then aligns his engorged cock with my tight ass and pushes into me with brutal force.

I gasp out loud as the dino stretches the limits of my toned body. His Jurassic cock fills me to the brim, yet I can't help but push my body back against him. We find a rhythm as he fucks me from behind and, the next thing I know, another creature steps out in front, shoving his dick down my throat. Now pinned between them, I'm helpless as the dinosaur lawyers take me from both ends. When the one behind me pushes forward, the one before me pushes back in time, pumping together within my body as I struggle to maintain their enormous shafts.

The most terrifying part, however, is how good it's starting to feel. By now, the fear has melted away into something else, a deep, aching arousal that swims through my blood in the most sensual way imaginable. Still on my hands and knees, I let one hand slip down across my stomach and onto my throbbing cock. The stimulation is almost too much to bear, but before I get a chance to cum I suddenly find myself being lifted off of the table in one of the monsters tiny T-rex arms.

One of the Tyrannosaurs has laid down across the dark oak in my place, his cock jutting out from his body like a thick, powerful tower of sex. With little I can do to stop it, I'm suddenly being lowered down onto him, facing away as my asshole draws closer and closer. I'm stopped briefly while the beast aligns himself at my tight backdoor. I try my best to relax, breathing deep in the clutches of the powerful monsters, but nothing I do could prepare me for the feeling of tightness as I'm slowly pushed down onto the dino's massive, pulsing cock.

I let out of cry of both pain and pleasure, reeling from his incredible girth as a penis substantially larger than the rest of the dinosaurs impales me. As my body reaches the hilt of his rod I lean back against him in near shock, moaning loudly while my eyes roll back into my head. It feels as though I'm being torn apart.

Of course, that's only the beginning of what these ancient monsters have in store for my ripped body. Almost immediately, the T-rex that had picked me up in the first place then positions himself in front of me. Two more of the prehistoric lawyers approach from either side and hold my legs back, spreading me open completely as I'm hammered up the ass from below. The T-rex in front of me aligns his cock with my already filled asshole and then pushes forward, forcefully stretching me as both cocks fill my hole in a powerful double penetration.

I let out a scream of passion, bracing myself as they slam into me. My body trembles with every thrust, stretched to the brink while I'm sandwiched between the two massive dinosaurs with my legs splayed wide.

"Fuck me harder!" I find myself commanding of my own violation. "Fuck the hell out of my tight ass with those big T-rex cocks!"

The monsters grunt and groan, obeying my commands to ram even harder.

"Is that all you've got?" I shriek, a fire in my eyes. "Treat me like the slutty fucking gay boy that I am."

They are absolutely throttling me now, bearing down with all of their reptilian power. I can feel myself drawing closer and closer to an orgasm as they pound me.

"Fuck me!" I yell, but the words are suddenly cut off as one of the tyrannosaurs that holds my leg decides to grab me by the head and stuff his cock down my throat. I gag on it, taken by surprise and trying desperately to center myself.

Suddenly, I'm completely lost in a mass of pounding erections and cold scaly flesh. I can't think straight, although I am vaguely aware of the Jurassic monsters trading positions within me, swapping places and making sure that everyone has a chance to ride my asshole. The aching sensation of cumming grows stronger and stronger now and I find myself reaching down to my cock to help my body along. I stroke myself rapidly, the sensation almost too much to bear until finally the feelings explode within me.

I gargle a frantic squeal around the cock in my throat and then quake with ecstasy, thrashing about while I'm debased in every hole. My stomach contracts tight, as if it's all I can do to hold myself together during the massive waves of sensation that course from head to toe. Hot ropes of semen eject from the end of my stiff rod.

Finally, after what feels like an eternity, the feelings pass and I collapse back onto the table in exhaustion. The T-rex lawyers remove themselves from my ass and mouth and then drag my limp body to the edge of the table, positioning me so that I'm bent over it with me feet on the ground and my ass in the air.

"Let's show this human what being tyrant lizards is all about!" One of them bellows.

My dino masters form a line behind me; the whole gang of them hard and ready to blow. The first in line steps up and then pushes his entire length deep into my asshole as a grit my teeth. He begins to pump in and out, steadily at first and then gaining speed as he plows me with his thickness. As his pounding reaches full tilt, the monster lets out a glorious roar and then erupts inside of me, spilling his hot prehistoric jizz up into the farthest reached of my ass. He pushes deep and holds, letting buckets of cum pump up into me before sliding out and letting his limp cock hang, white liquid following closely behind as it runs down my legs in thick streaks.

The next dinosaur quickly takes his place, throttling my tight hole in the same fashion until he pops, as well. The T-rex roars loudly and ejects his semen into my asshole, letting it mix with the load before it.

This continues down the line until all of the ancient creatures have emptied their payloads inside of me, a creamy mixture of dinosaur seed that covers my ass, legs and the floor beneath. When they are all finally finish, I fall back into the chair behind me; naked, ravaged and full of cum.

The next morning I arrive at work early and head straight to my desk, rejuvenated and ready to take on the day. I've got a lot of papers to file, so I might as well dive right in and get it done.

Strangely though, when I show up all of the paperwork has been taken care of. I check to make sure this is actually my desk, and it is, so I sit down in my chair and suddenly find myself with nothing to work on.

The night before is a total haze, a mixture of reality and gay dinosaur nightmare that I can't quite fully sort out yet.

Suddenly, the mail guy appears out of nowhere. It was too good to be true, I think to myself, preparing for the worst.

He makes his way down the row of desks, dropping off stack after stack of paperwork that needs to be filed while I flinch with the sight of every new delivery. When the mail guy finally reaches my desk there is nothing in his basket but a single letter with my name written across the front in red pen. It's marked with a strange wax seal displaying the name 'Tyson Rex'. I open it.

The first thing that falls out is a small card, which reads, 'It was a pleasure doing business with you. Looking forward to working late again. – Tyson'

Suddenly, I'm in complete shock. I stare down at the final contents of the envelope; a check for ten million dollars.

SPACE RAPTOR BUTT INVASION

"It's gonna be a long year for you up here." My fellow astronaut, Officer Pike, says. "You think you're ready for it?"

"Ready as I'll ever be." I tell him with a slight smile.

I lean back in my chair and watch as Pike continues to pack his bags, preparing for his launch home that looms just a few hours away. Lucky bastard.

Nothing can quite prepare you for the loneliness of space until you're actually here, floating in orbit on a giant rock as it circles some distant star.

Pike knows this as well as I do, we were both stationed here on Zorbus two years ago, taking over for two other astronauts who had just finished putting in their time. This would probably give me some sort of solace, knowing that Pike fully understood the feelings of loneliness that were already brewing up inside of me, but even given our shared experiences he has no idea what's in store.

This is because, up until today, all astronauts participating in the Earth Outpost Program have had a partner with them at all times. In fact, some of the more active stations can have up to six humans inhabiting them at once.

Now, thanks to budget cuts, our tiny little station on Zorbus will have one single resident for then next year; yours truly. This is not at all what I signed up for, but at this point I'm not exactly in the position to argue.

"Just remember," Pike says with complete sincerity, "You're up here doing a lot of good for the folks back down there on earth. Try not to forget it."

I let out a long sigh. "I know, I know."

Pike stops. "I don't think you do and I don't blame you. It's easy to get detached up here, Lance, but you've gotta focus on the positives. Without us, earth would have no hope of ever finding another home, I mean how many years do we have left down there, even with population control?"

"Ten, max." I tell him. This was the current scientific concurrence on Earth's lifespan, a dreadful thought. "I know you're right, but what is it helping to have me just sit out here like this. We already know that there's not enough oxygen on this rock to sustain life."

Pike smiles. "But there could be! There is hope here and you know that."

I shake my head. "I don't know man, we've been terraforming this dust for five years an we're no better off than when we started." I wave an arm behind me, motioning towards the massive glass window of the space station.

The entire wall is translucent, showing off a truly breathtaking view of a hilly grey landscape beyond where two separate moons hang brilliantly in the dark sky. If I hadn't seen this view every morning for far longer than I'd care to remember, I might even be moved to tears by the sight, a real manifestation of mankind's commitment to science and space travel.

Instead, I find myself bored, reminded that as Pike is taking off in his shuttle pod towards earth, I'm going to be trekking back across the massive grey dunes to gather data from the terraforming station.

"You know it could be much worse." Pike offers. "In station sixteen on Kerlin they don't even have a gravity drive."

I'm in shock. "You mean they've just been… floating around in there?"

"Basically." Pike says. "At least you get to pretend you're on earth until you head outside."

I suppose I'm looking for any assurance that I can get at this point, because somehow Pike's words actually make me feel a little bit better. I guess it's not that bad up here.

"You wanna play one last game of ping pong before you go?" I ask. "We can turn the gravity low just like you like it."

Pike cracks a wry grin. "You're on."

I begin to stand when suddenly an announcement comes blaring over the space station's loudspeakers in that same mechanical voice that I've come to know and love. "Shuttle Five Alpha has arrived. Officer Pike is now dismissed."

Pike shrugs. "Guess I've gotta roll."

As Pike puts on his space suit I join him, figuring that I'll walk out to see him off and then continue on my way to the terraforming outpost. We suit up quicker than normal as, clearly, Pike can't wait to get off of this fucking rock, and then open the hatch door and step out into the dark, alien landscape.

"Well, I'll be seeing you soon I guess." Officer Pike radios to me through his helmet, exchanging a hug in our bulky white space suits.

"Yeah you will." I tell him. "In one year I'll buy you a beer back on Earth."

"Sounds like a plan." Pike says.

The officer walks over to his shuttle pod and punches in a few numbers on the keypad, then steps back as the door lifts open. The dust is still settling from the ships recent landing in this low gravity air.

"Fly safe." I offer through the static of our space suit headsets.

Pike nods and is about to close his shuttle door but then stops, looking at me with a deathly seriousness. "All joking aside," he says. "Don't think too hard out here, stay light."

I give Pike a strange look, not quite fully understanding what he means.

"Space can get a little strange." Pike tells me. "People can start seeing things…" He trails off. "Anyway, just take care of yourself."

"I will." I say with a nod.

Pike closes the shuttle door and then begins his countdown for launch, prompting me to step back away from the ship. Moments later the entire thing starts to lift up into the air, propelled by its minor gravity drive, and before I know it the shuttle is hurtling off through space so fast that I can barely see it.

Suddenly, I am completely alone.

Still haunted by Pike's final words, I begin to make my usual walk across the hills of space dust, towards our perpetually worthless terraforming station.

As much as I've gotten used to the sight of these alien vistas, I will admit that it still makes me a little giddy every time that I go for a walk in such a low gravity environment. As I bound over the hills, I'll admit that a smile slowly begins to cross my face.

It's only when I reach the top of the mount and look down the other side that I freeze in shock and fear. There before me, some hundred yards away, is the terraforming station, just as it should be. Beyond the station, however, is a figure that's clad in a space suit quite similar to mine.

The two of us seem to notice each other at almost exactly the same time, locked in a bizzare stand off before, suddenly, the other figure turns and climbs aboard its two wheeled vehicle. The next thing I know, the space suited figure is taking off into the distance, riding furiously down into an alien valley before disappearing from my sight.

It all happens so quickly that I don't even have time to give chase, simply struck dumb as I reel with the significance of what just happened.

"Holy shit." Is all that I can manage to say.

As I continue towards the terraforming station my head is swimming with kinds of confusing thoughts. Was I already space crazy? Was I so upset by the thought of my impending loneliness that I'd created a fellow astronaut in my head?

It's possible. Yet, as I arrive at the station and search the surrounding grounds, I find definite footprints and wheel tracks in the dust.

Unfortunately, as the space winds begin to pick up, I quickly realize that I will not be able to follow them before they are swept away entirely.

I quickly fulfill my duties at the outpost and then immediately head back towards the main station, wasting no time at all as I head inside and tear off my space suit.

"Computer, has earth sent another astronaut to join me?" I ask aloud.

"No, you will spend the next year alone." The space station computer says, its mechanical voice echoing throughout the massive outpost.

"Are you sure, because I could have sworn that I just saw someone out there at the terraforming unit." I continue.

"I am sure." States the computer flatly. "There are no records of any new arrivals at this station."

I collapse onto the couch and look out at my tired and true view of the alien landscape, letting out a long sigh. "Then who the fuck was out there tonight?" I ask myself.

I awaken to the sound of a loud knocking on the hatch door, and then sit upright in a frantic moment of confusion.

"Pike?" I call out, glancing around as I try to get my bearings. I must have fallen asleep on the couch.

It only takes me a few seconds to remember that Pike is no longer here with me, and a stab of fear comes shooting through my heart. If not Pike knocking on the door, than who is it? Cautiously, I stand up and walk over to the hatch, wondering now if the sound was nothing more than my paranoid mind playing tricks on me.

The knocking comes again and I jump.

"Hello?" I call out.

Three more knocks.

My curiosity getting the best of me, I press a few buttons on the keypad to open the external hatch. Fortunately, there is a camera set up right inside the holding area and I gasp aloud as I see that same, spacesuit-wearing figure enter the chamber.

"Hello?" I say into the microphone next to me as the external door closes behind the astronaut. "Who are you."

"Who are *you*?" Comes a voice from beneath the helmet.

"Lance Tanner of the Earth Outpost Program." I offer.

"Earth?" Asks the voice from inside the space suit.

"Yes." I tell him.

The voice starts to laugh, quietly at first and then in a loud, jovial tone. "We should talk." Says the astronaut. "May I come in?"

I'm not exactly sure what the right call is here, but I can't just have this strange spaceman standing in my hatch all day and I'm more than a little anxious to get to the bottom of all this. I sigh and then reluctantly open the inside hatch door.

Suddenly, I'm standing face to face with the unknown spaceman.

"Lance, nice to meet you." I say, extending my hand.

The figure extends a gloved hand as well, which I immediately notice has only three fingers. "I'm Orion." The figure responds. "And likewise."

There's a loud hiss as the window of his helmet slides upwards and I gasp aloud, recoiling in shock. There beneath the tinted glass is the smiling face of a voracious velociraptor, one of the most feared dinosaurs to ever roam the earth.

"But you're... You're a..." I stammer.

"A dinosaur?" Asks the beast. "Yes."

I feel faint, suddenly completely convinced that I'm suffering from some kind of severe space delusion. "But, that makes no sense." I say.

"I agree," Says the raptor. "I was told that this planet was entirely uninhabited."

"Who told you that?" I ask, shocked.

"The raptor scientists back on Earth Two." The prehistoric beast responds flatly.

This is too much to take in all at once. My head throbbing with anxiety, I step backwards and then have a seat on the couch once again. "This can't be real." I start to repeat over and over again. "This can't be real. This can't be real."

"I can assure you that I'm very real." Says Orion.

"Then what the fuck are you talking about?!" I shout, finally losing it. "What is Earth Two?"

The raptor astronaut nods in understanding. "Ah yes, I can see where the confusion could come from. I'm assuming that back on Earth One you were taught that my people died in some kind of ice age? Something like that?"

I nod.

The dinosaur chuckles. "That's some revisionist history for you. No, there was no ice age. The real reason that the dinosaurs aren't around anymore is because we all left, in search of a larger and more forgiving planet than Earth One. We sailed the stars for many years until finding a suitable home on Earth Two, but we still like to keep tabs on all parts of the galaxy."

"Is that what you're doing here?" I ask.

The dinosaur nods. "Yep. All alone in an empty solar system."

As Orion says this I detect a deep sadness behind his eyes, something that I can relate with all too well.

"Well..." I start, not exactly sure where I'm headed. "I mean, we're both up here together, I can't see why we can't hang out a bit."

I see a faint glimmer of hope behind Orion's dinosaur expression. "Yeah?" He asks.

"Sure. You play ping pong?"

Over the next few days Orion continues to come by the station and hang out. The two of us are an incredible duo, talking for hours on end about our experiences in space or trading nostalgic stories about our home worlds. Despite being a bloodthirsty dinosaur carnivore, Orion is actually incredibly sweet and has a truly gentle soul. The longer that we spend together, the more I find myself drawn to him, attracted even. Our difference in species surely couldn't classify me as gay, could it?

As they days turn into weeks, and weeks into months, I begin to wonder if I'd even care.

Finally, after a long night of ping pong and chowing down on astronaut ice cream, me and Orion find ourselves lounging on the couch and looking out over the grey hills together.

"Can I ask you a personal question?" I start, watching the dinosaur from the corner of my eye.

Orion smiles. "Sure thing, Lance. Shoot."

"You ever think about what it would be like to fuck a human." I ask. My heart is now thumping ferociously in my chest, but I try to remain calm and even keeled.

"Yeah, I mean, who hasn't?" Orion offers. "The thing is, I'm a pretty big dinosaur and human women are just to delicate. I would probably crush one if I tried."

I let his words linger in the air for a moment, not sure if I should say what I so desperately want to. But it's now or never, I think to myself, taking a deep breath.

"What about a human *man*?" I question.

I can see the raptors expression suddenly change as understanding washes over him. "Yeah, I think I might be into that actually." Orion tells me.

"I mean, it's not gay if it's a dude raptor and a dude human, right?" I ask.

"Totally not gay." Says the dinosaur. "The raptor would have to be in control though; dominating, even."

"Yeah." I sigh, my cock rock hard in my pants.

There's a moment of silence.

"Get down on your knees." The raptor suddenly commands.

Seizing the moment I follow his instructions, slipping off of the couch and crawling onto my hands and knees in front of him. I sit with my head at the level of Orion's lap and look up with my big brown eyes.

"Unzip me." Orion instructs.

I shaking as I slowly reach up and pull down the zipper of his space pants, where a massive red dino cock is just waiting to be unleashed from its fabric prison.

"Take it out." Orion demands. "You need to be punished for being such a filthy little... human."

"I am a filthy little human." I repeat, coyly, then pull down the waistband of his space briefs and remove Orion's enormous raptor rod. I grip it tightly and then start to pump my firm grip up and down over his length.

Orion leans back into his chair, reeling from the incredible sensation of my touch. I start slowly at first and then gain speed until I find a pleasant rhythm, using both hands to fully service his huge scaly cock.

"Do you like that?" I ask. "How does it feel to punish your astronaut human sex toy?"

"Oh my god, that's so amazing." Orion moans, placing his claws around the back of my head and pulling me closer to him. "Now let me punish that pretty gay mouth of yours."

I open wide as Orion guides me over the end of his shaft, pushing keep into my mouth as I wrap my lips tightly around the girth of his dick. He keeps forcing me deeper and deeper until finally his swollen cock hits the back of my gag reflex and I retch loudly, pulling back and releasing his member from my throat. I cough and sputter a bit, trying to collect myself as salty tears stream down my face.

"You're gonna take that dinosaur dick and you're gonna like it." Orion tells me, taking me by the head and thrusting me down again. "You should have known better than to test me. My people have been fucking for billions of years before you humans we were even around."

This time I'm ready for his length, however, and as the head of his cock hits my gag reflex I somehow manage to relax enough to let him pass. Now without a limit to his dominating deep throat, Orion pushes me down until my head is pressed deep into his lap, my eyes and nose forced up against his rock hard reptile abs. Orion holds me here for a moment, enjoying the sensation of being entirely consumed within my throat, and then finally pulls me back and begins to pump my head up and down over his shaft.

When Orion finally lets me up for air I take a massive gasp and then climb up to kiss him deeply on the mouth. I reach down between my legs and grab his now slippery dick in my hand, beating it rapidly while using the leftover spit from my mouth as lube.

"Pound me like the homo spaceboy that I am." I beg.

Orion smiles as I say this, then reaches up and pulls my shirt off over my head. My space pants and underwear come down over next, completely exposing myself to the raptor.

"Do you want to fuck me?" I ask.

Suddenly, Orion stands up from the couch and grabs me by the arms, spinning me around and tossing me down onto the cushion in his place.

"I'm the one that decides who gets fucked around here." He says, slapping me hard on the ass.

I'm leaned over the couch now, facing away from him with my muscular gay butt popped out in the air as Orion saddles up behind me and begins to align his member with my puckered asshole. Seconds later, Orion is pushing forward into me, testing the limits of my aching tightness.

I let out a long moan of pleasure as he fills me up, gripping hard onto the back of the chair in front of me. "Oh fuck, you're the best dinosaur bud a guy could ask for." I whimper. "Discipline me, I need it."

Orion starts to push in and out of me, slowly at first and the gaining speed with each successive swoop until finally he's pounding into me at a steady pace, shaking the couch beneath me with every slam against my ass. I reach back with both hands and spread myself open for him, so that he can get a good look at the toned young body he's railing.

"Do you like what you see?" I ask playfully, looking back over my shoulder at the strong, ancient beast as he rams me.

Orion reaches forward and grabs me by the base of my hair with his claw, pulling me back towards him as he continues to rail me from behind. "Take this dick and shut your mouth." He commands. "The dinosaur is dishing out the punishment here, so the humans don't get to ask questions."

"Yes, sir." I answer meekly.

"What the fuck was that?" Orion counters.

"Yes, sir!" I say a little louder.

"Good." Orion tells me. He's pounding me as hard as he can now, the force of our fucking literally scooting the couch across the space station floor.

I can feel the pleasant sensation of a prostate orgasm blossoming deep within me, simmering to a boil of pleasure that makes me tremble with anticipation. I reach down and play with my dick to help myself along, edging closer and closer until I'm just about ready to erupt when suddenly Orion pulls out and flips me over.

I'm laying on my back in the couch now with my legs spread wide, completely open and exposed like that filthy gay boy that I am.

Orion climbs forward towards me a bit, using the couch as leverage while he aligns his cock with my ass and then thrusts forward. I let out a long groan of pleasure as he pulses within my depths, holding my ripped legs back while I quake with wild passion.

"I can't believe I'm doing this." I mumble, and then start to frantically repeat over and over again. "I can't believe I'm doing this, I can't believe I'm fucking doing this."

The more the feelings of orgasm grow within me, the more I feel as though I'm moving towards a state of real shock. The events of the evening are catching up with me and suddenly I find myself in a blissed out sexual trance. I start to frantically stroke my dick and moments later the powerful sensation of orgasm explodes within me.

I kick my legs out straight as my stomach clenches tight in a series of mighty spasms, gritting my teeth as the words "Oh fuck" force their way through them in a tense hiss. Moments later, A second wave of ecstasy hits me and suddenly I'm throwing my head back and howling with pleasure, unable to contain the sensations that explode through my body. My cum splatters everywhere.

Orion doesn't let up for a second, pummeling my tight asshole with everything that he's got while I cum hard. When the waves of pleasure finally subside he grabs me around the waist and lifts me up into the air, putting an arm under each leg so that he's completely in control of my movements. He lowers me down and suddenly I find myself being pumped forcefully over Orion's hard dinosaur shaft, my muscular frame brutally impaled onto his thickness as I cry out for more.

"Fuck me harder!" I scream. "Use that tight ass with your big raptor dick!"

Kick slams me as hard as he can onto his rod, the muscles in his scaled arms rippling with every movement.

"You've been a very bad astronaut." Orion tells me, his raptor face pressed hard against mine as we pump together in sweaty unison. "So you're gonna take my Jurassic load up your asshole and you're gonna like it."

"Yes, sir." I tell him. "Fill me with that hot load."

"Beg me!" Orion demands.

"Please fill me with your nasty dino load!" I cry out. "I want your jizz inside of me!"

"More!" He screams in my face. "Tell me to fucking cum!"

"Blow your load inside of me!" I answer back with equal fervor.

The pace quickens to an incredible speed, Orion slamming up into my butthole like a jackhammer as I hang in the air before him. Moments later, he leans back his head and lets out a powerful roar while pushing deep and holding.

"I'm cumming!" Orion yells, his thick dick erupting within me. I can feel his warm jizz spill up into my tightness in a series of commanding ejections, his cock twitching hard with every load until my entire asshole is filled. When there's no room left his spunk comes spilling out from the edges and onto the space station floor in a splatter of pearly white.

The raptor holds me in the air like this for a minute while we both catch our breath and then slowly lowers me down to the ground, where I stand on woozy legs.

"Fuck, that was incredible." Orion tells me, clearly just as exhausted as I am.

"I think that the next year up here is going to work out just fine." I tell the dinosaur, unable to keep the smile from spreading out across my face as I lay back against the soft couch behind me

ABOUT THE AUTHOR

Dr. Chuck Tingle is an erotic author and Tae Kwon Do grandmaster (almost black belt) from Billings, Montana. After receiving his PhD at DeVry University in holistic massage, Chuck found himself fascinated by all things sensual, leading to his creation of the "tingler", a story so blissfully erotic that it cannot be experienced without eliciting a sharp tingle down the spine.

Chuck's hobbies include backpacking, checkers and sport.

Made in the USA
San Bernardino, CA
09 February 2015